THE
COWDOG.

THE CASE OF THE
NIGHT-STALKING BONE MONSTER

Hank THE COWDOG®

THE CASE OF THE NIGHT-STALKING BONE MONSTER

John R. Erickson

Illustrations by Gerald L. Holmes

Maverick Books
Published by Gulf Publishing Company
Houston, Texas

Maverick Books
Published by Gulf Publishing Company
P.O. Box 2608, Houston, Texas 77252-2608

10 9 8 7 6 5 4 3 2 1

ISBN 0-87719-310-X

Printed in the United States of America.

Hank the Cowdog is a registered trademark of John R. Erickson.

For Dean Willis,
a young friend and Hank fan,
who was badly injured in a car accident and is
fighting for his life in an Amarillo hospital.
Blessings, Dean.

C O N T E N T S

C H A P T E R
1
THE INCREDIBLE
REINDEER SNOUTS

It's me again, Hank the Cowdog. Do you believe in Bone Monsters? Neither did I, until one struck our ranch and made off with my fortune in buried bones, and then I had no choice but to believe in them.

Bone Monsters, that is. I had always believed in bones. Who wouldn't believe in bones? They're one of the things that give meaning to a dog's life. I love bones, always have. They're wonderful.

Bone Monsters, on the other hand, aren't wonderful and I don't love 'em. They're very scary, as you will see if you should happen to work up the courage to read this story.

And let me warn you right here: Don't tackle this story unless you've completed a course in Monster Safety, because . . . well, I don't know what might happen. Something bad.

Bedwetting. A runny nose. Heat rash. Pulmonary Brouhaha.

You've been warned. Proceed with caution.

It all began, as I recall, around the middle of March. No,the middle of April, and I can pin it down to the very exact day. It was the fourteenth of April.

I happened to be sitting near the front gate, facing east. I had barked up the sun at precisely seven o'clock. After performing that very important duty, I lingered near the front gate to do a Turkey Patrol. Whilst I was barking up the sun, don't you see, my ears began picking up unusual signals from a chinaberry grove near the creek.

I stopped—froze, actually—I stopped and froze, twisted my head from side to side, and initiated the Sound Detection Procedure. I went to Full Lift-Up on both Earatory Scanners and began monitoring the entire electromagical spectrum.

I was listening for turkey sounds, see. At that hour of the morning, they often make sounds. They gobble. And they make another sound, too, which I can't reproduce because I'm not a turkey. It's kind of a squawk or a cluck.

I picked up the sounds, just as clear as a bell. Those turkeys were down there in the chinaberry grove, squawking and gobbling, and little did they know that I was spying on them and picking up every word of their conversation.

Would you like to peek at a transcript of this monitoring session? Ordinarily we don't release this information to the general public because . . . well, because we don't. It's classified information, see, and we usually withhold these transcripts for twenty-five years because . . .

Well, because we do, and that's reason enough. We do it because we do it. If we didn't, we wouldn't.

But if you want to peek at one of the Turkey Transcripts, I can't see that it would hurt anything.

Ready? Here we go.

OFFICIAL SECRET TRANSCRIPT

Turkey Monitoring Operations:
Codename "Starfish Sandwich"
East Yard Gate Station
April 14

Turkey 1: "Gobble, gobble, gobble."
Turkey 2: "Cluck, cluck."
Turkey 3: "Squawk, screek."
Turkey 1: "Gobble?"

Turkey 3: "Cluck, squawk."

Turkey 2: "Cluck, cluck, screek."

Turkey 1: "Gobble, gobble, gobble."

Turkey 2: "Cluck."

END OF SECRET TRANSCRIPT

So there you are. Pretty impressive, huh? Those birds might as well have been in the movies, the way we had 'em covered. We knew all their secrets, their plans, everything. We knew what they were thinking before they even thought it.

Of course, the problem with turkeys is that they don't do much thinking about anything, which makes their conversations a little on the dull side.

Pretty boring, actually.

I wouldn't want to spend too much of my time monitoring turkeys.

Anyways, I was at the Turkey Wire, doing my job, when all at once I heard a vehicle approaching from the north. Unidentified Vehicles get an automatic override in our defense system, which means that at the first sound of a UV, all Turkey Traffic is blacked out so that we can sound the alarm.

I left my post at the gate . . . not the gate post but my position near the gate post . . . I left my post at the gate post . . .

Phooey. I left the gate and never mind the post and went ripping out to intercept the . . .

Okay, relax. It was Slim's pickup, which no doubt contained Slim. Slim was the driver, see, and once I had established this fact, I switched all circuits from Emergency Red to Routine Blue, and provided Slim with an escort all the way to . . .

That was odd. Instead of driving down to the corrals, where he usually went at this hour of the morning, he stopped in front of the house.

The moment he stepped out of the pickup, I was there to greet him. I gave him Broad Wags and Joyful Leaps, just to let him know that, by George, it was sure good to see him again.

That should have been enough to start his day off right, but yikes, he looked at me with a pair of stony eyes and said, "What are you so happy about, pooch? Don't you know what day this is?"

Well, I . . . no, I didn't. Up until that very moment, I had thought it was a fairly normal day. Obviously, I had missed something.

He shoved his hands into his jeans pockets and trudged up to the front door. He carried a bundle of something under his arm, a mess of papers, it appeared. His back was bent and his head was low, as though he were packing several sacks of feed, only he wasn't.

He tapped on the door. Loper appeared. He was not smiling too. "Come in," was all he said. The door closed behind them.

My goodness, this was a dark day. Something bad was happening on my ranch, and I didn't even know what it was.

(You probably think it had something to do with the Night-Stalking Bone Monster, but I'll give you a hint: It didn't, not yet. That came later.)

I had planned to move along and do a routine sweep of the entire headquarters area, but it was clear by then that we had a serious problem on the ranch, and I needed to remain on call until we cleared it up.

After marking two of Slim's tires—I saw no real need to mark all four of them; I mean, we knew the vehicle and a Short Mark was good enough—after the so-forth, I curled up beside the front gate and . . . snork, mirk . . . perhaps I dozed off for a moment or two.

The next thing I knew, they were coming down the sidewalk. Slim and Loper, that is. "Get out of the gate, Hank." I leaped to my feet, staggered three steps to the north, and did a quick scan of their faces. They were still dark, depressed, angry.

The sun had climbed fairly high above the horizon. Perhaps I had dozed for an hour or two instead of a moment or two.

They came through the gate. Instead of doing Joyous Leaps and Broad Wags, I switched all circuits over to Graveyard Mode. If they were depressed, I was depressed. If they were sad, so was I. That's just part of being a loyal dog.

Fellers, we were sad and depressed. Perhaps we were going to climb into Slim's pickup and drive to a funeral. Yes, this was a very sad . . . only they didn't climb into the pickup. They started walking north, towards the county road.

Now, that was strange. These two cowboys weren't fond of walking, yet here they were . . . walking. It was hard to believe, but I fell in step beside them. We walked in silence. Oh, and did I mention that each of them carried a white envelope? Yes, they did.

At last, Slim spoke. "Well, here goes another year down the drain. You reckon we'll ever find happiness again?"

"Oh sure. Fools always forget. Give us six months and we'll be able to smile again. By Christmas, we'll be laughing."

"I ain't so sure. I think my giggle box is permanently broke, and so am I."

"Well, look at it this way, Slim. If you had that money, you'd spend it on something foolish."

"I'd sure try."

"Yeah, me too. But I guess Sally May didn't need that new dress."

"Nope. And I didn't need to get these boots half-soled."

"Heck no. Wear a thicker sock."

"I sure hope this check don't bounce."

"They'll be in touch, don't worry."

"I'll bet."

None of this made any sense to me. As near as I could figure it, Slim had worn out all his socks and was sending off an order for more. He hoped they would arrive by Christmas, and if they did, he would . . . laugh, I guess.

Sounded crazy to me.

By that time we had reached the mailbox, which appeared to be our destination. Ah ha, yes. The pieces of the puzzle were falling into place. Loper opened the little door and pitched his letter inside.

"Well, back to work."

Slim held his letter up and gave it a pat. "Here we are, little feller. Go find the IRS and tell 'em that

8

they've ruined my life—again." He pitched his letter inside and slammed the door.

We trudged back down to the house. There, we split up and went our separate ways: Loper into the house; Slim to the corrals; and me to the gas tanks.

And you know what? I never did figure out what we were all being so sad about. What the heck was an IRS?

International Reserve of Socks?

Interplanetary Rhubarb Society?

Incredible Reindeer Snouts?

I decided to stop worrying about it. If you can't figure out why you're miserable, maybe you're not.

I had more important things to worry about, such as . . . well, you'll soon find out.

CHAPTER

2

THE CAT TRIES TO STEAL MY T-BONES

I couldn't help feeling just a little angry that I had wasted the best part of the morning trying to be a good dog and showing sympathy for my cowboy pals.

I mean, we try to help them out and share their little sorrows, but there's a limit to how sad a dog can feel about holey socks and reindeer snouts. Down deep, where it really counts, I just don't care about either subject.

I'm sorry.

And I was way behind in my work and beginning to feel the awesome weight of responsibility that came with my job. Running a ranch is no cup of worms, let me tell you, and I still had eighteen hours of work to do before I slept.

11

I hurried past the front gate, headed down the caliche hill, past that cottonwood tree that was just beginning to put out a few spring leaves, past the . . .

Suddenly I heard a sound. A voice. A child's voice. Little Alfred's voice, to be exact, and here's what he said: "Hee-oo, kitty kitty. Hee-oo, Petie. Come for scwaps."

I went to Full Air Brakes and skidded to a stop. Scwaps? My ears shot up to Full and Undivided Attention, for you see, I had just broken the code of a very important transmission. You probably weren't aware of this, but "scwaps" in Kid Language means "scraps" to the rest of us.

My goodness, I had just stumbled into a conspiracy of major portions. It appeared that Little Alfred, who or whom I had always considered my special pal, was about to offer delicious scraps to my least favorite character on the ranch: Pete the Cheat, Pete the Sneaking Little Barncat.

I was stunned, shocked beyond recognition. Wounded. Devustated . . . devvusstated . . . davastated . . . deeply hurt, shall we say.

Gee whiz, Alfred and I had been through SO MUCH together, yet now he had turned against his very best friend in the whole world and was about to offer MY scraps to the cat!

Oh, pain! Oh, treachery! Oh, broken heart!

A lot of your ordinary dogs would have quit right there—admitted defeat and gone into mourning for several days. Not me. "Ordinary" has never been a word that applied to me.

Hey, my special friendship with Alfred was worth fighting for, and . . . okay, maybe the scraps were too, especially since the villain in this case was Kitty Kitty.

Would I lie down and roll over and let the cat corrupt my long and meaningful friendship with Little Alfred? No sir. I would fight for my rights. I would fight for Truth and Justice and Friendship and Scrap Rights.

Kitty was in big trouble.

I squared my enormous shoulders and rumbled off towards the yard gate. I could see him standing there—the boy, not the cat—I could see him standing there. He held a plate in his left hand. He was grinning.

He would be shocked, of course, that I had intercepted his secret call to Mister Kitty Moocher. No doubt he had called the cat in a soft voice, hoping that we dogs would miss it. Ha! Little did he know the range and scope of our listening devicers. The same instruments that spy on turkeys can pick up the tiniest of whispers about scraps.

And so it was that I stormed over to the yard gate and broke up this shabby little conspiracy before it ever got started.

Our eyes met. Through tail wags and other modes of expression, I said to him: "Alfred, I'm shocked that you would try to hold a secret Scrap Time without consulting me. And furthermore . . . "

He cut off my furthermore with a laugh. "Hi, Hankie. I knew that if I called for the kitty, you'd come. I fooled ya, didn't I, Hankie?"

HUH?

I, uh, hardly knew how to respond. My mind was racing. My data banks whirred as I tried to make sense of his . . .

I mean, who'd ever think that an innocent child might put out false information and phony calls? If you can't trust the kids, who or whom can you trust? And what's the world coming to?

I, uh, went to Slow Wags and squeezed up a grin which said,"Hey, pal, we were on to your tricks from the very beginning. We suspected that you were operating in Backwards Code, and we just played along with it to, uh . . . what's on the plate?"

I lifted my nose and gave the air a sniffing. My goodness,when the readout came in from Data Control, we found ourselves, well, shaking with excitement, you might say, because our sensory devices had picked up fragrant waves.

Holy smokes, the kid was holding a plate of STEAK BONES!

He widened his eyes and dropped his voice to a whisper. "Hankie, guess what I've got on the pwate. Steak bones. Juicy yummy steak bones."

Yes, we, uh, our intelligence sources had already . . . could we hurry this up a bit?

"You want a bone?"

Well, I . . . yes, a bone would be nice. Or two or three. Or, to make things simple, maybe all of them.

He lifted a bone off the plate and waved it in front of my nose. Holy tamales, that was a fresh T-bone, saved from supper the night before! And have we discussed T-bones? I love 'em, absolutely love 'em, and oftentimes I dream about 'em at night, is how much I love 'em.

He continued to wave the bone around in front of my nose. The fragrant waves of steakness filled my nostrils. My mouth began to water. I licked my chops and hopped up on my back legs, but the little scamp pulled the bone out of my reach. And laughed.

Why was he doing this? I mean, he had a bone and I wanted a bone, so why couldn't we cut a deal and be done with it? Before I could answer that question, I suddenly realized that we had been joined by a third party.

Pete.

Pete had raised his worthless carcass out of his bed in Sally May's iris patch and had come slinking into our mists—grinning, purring, and holding his tail straight up in the air.

The mere sight of him caused my lips to rise into a snarl, for you see, I don't like cats.

"Pete, for your own safety, I must advise you not to come any closer."

"Hmmmm. Well, hello, Hankie."

"Hello yourself, Kitty, and also goodbye. You're walking into a potentially deadly situation here and you'd best leave."

"Oh really?" He slithered through the yard gate, rubbed on the gate post, and then began rubbing on my front legs. "I could have sworn that Little Alfred was calling me to scraps, Hankie."

"Wrong, Kitty. He was using Backwards Code, which means that he used your name as a code word to call me."

16

"Hmmmmm, how interesting. I've never heard of Backwards Code before."

"Of course not. You're only a cat and cats know nothing about Security Work and the many codes we use."

"It sounds very complicated, Hankie."

"It's complicated beyond your wildest imagination, Kitty, but the bottom line is pretty simple."

"Oh really?" He grinned up at me and continued rubbing on my legs, which drives me nuts. "What is the bottom line, Hankie? I can't wait to hear."

"The bottom line is that these are my scraps. You got that? MY SCRAPS. Goodbye."

"But Hankie, if Alfred was using Backwards Code, then surely that means that the scraps are mine." He fluttered his eyelids. "Backwards Code makes everything backwards, right?"

I cut my eyes from side to side. This was a new sneaky trick and just for a moment it caught me unprepared. At last Data Control provided me with an answer.

"Pete, that's the stupidest thing I ever heard. And stop rubbing on my legs."

"No, it's not stupid, Hankie. Backwards Code makes everything backwards, so if Alfred said, 'Pete, come for scraps,' what he really meant was, 'Hankie, come for NO scraps.'"

Obviously this was no ordinary dumb cat. He was a clever ordinary dumb cat, and I had to be careful. He was trying to lure me into a trap.

Of course, there was no chance that he would succeed. I had vast experience in beating cats at their shabby little games. It was just a matter of framing up a tightly reasoned, highly logical answer to his ridiculous argument.

But before I could get that done, Little Alfred pushed the bone—MY fresh juicy T-bone—in front of the cat's nose. Pete's eyes widened, and the rest was just what you would expect from a greedy cat.

He dug his claws and sank his teeth into my bone, cut loose with a warning yowl, pinned back his ears, and began glaring ice picks at me.

Well, you know me. Do unto others but don't take trash off the cats. My patients were wearing thin.

My patients were wearing thin clothes.

My patients were growing thin.

Whatever. I was getting angry.

"Excuse me, Kitty, but you seem to have lost your mind, and you're fixing to lose parts of your body if you don't unhand my bone. Drop it, Pete. Reach for the sky."

His yowling increased in volume, and then he HISSED at me. He shouldn't have done that. Nothing inflames a dog quite as much as hissing. It's like throwing gasoline on a fire ant.

My ears shot up. My lips rose in a deadly snarl. A growl began to rumble in my throat. And then . . .

CHAPTER

3

MY BONES VANISH

Out of the corner of my eye, I caught a glimpse of Little Alfred. He was wearing a huge grin and his eyes were sparkling like . . . I don't know what. Diamonds, I suppose.

But the point is that he looked very happy about something, and all at once the pieces of the puzzle began falling into place.

The little snipe was bored and had drawn me and Kitty down into a show . . . into a showdown, I should say. In other words, he wanted us to fight over the bone. In other words, Pete and I were being used.

This threw an entirely different light on the whole situation. I turned back to the cat.

"Pete, I've just figgered this deal out. Alfred is trying to promote a fight between us. That was his purpose in using Backwards Code, to foment jealousy and envy and greed between us. Just look at yourself, Pete. He's succeeded."

He stopped yowling and listened.

I continued. "He's appealing to our lowest instincts, Pete, and has brought us to the brink of open warfare. I don't know about you, but I kind of resent being used by a bratty little kid.

"I mean, we're adult dogs and cats, yet we're being tooled around by this ornery little stinkpot. I've got no grudge against you, Pete, and I think it would be a crying shame for us to go into combat over something as silly as a bone. What's a bone, Pete? The world's full of bones. This is just one of thousands, millions.

"And I ask you, Pete, sincerely and from my deepest heart: Is one measly bone worth all this? Just look what it's done to you. You've turned into a greedy, selfish, miserly little brute."

He still had his teeth sunk into my . . . into the, uh, bone. I continued.

"I don't know about you, Pete, but I'm ashamed of myself, and I'm ashamed of yourself too. I mean, we have every reason to be friends. We share the same ranch, the same world, the same stars at night. Yet here we are, at each other's throats over a . . . over a paltry, insignificant little bone.

"Talk to me, Pete, tell me what you think. Am I right or wrong about this? I sincerely and honestly want to know your thoughts on this."

He dropped the bone. "Well, Hankie, since you put it that way . . . "

Heh, heh. In one rapid motion, I snatched up my bone and buried Kitty beneath an avalanche of paws and claws. He never saw it coming and he never had a chance.

Okay, maybe he didn't stay buried under the avalanche for very long, and maybe he cut loose with a burst of fully-automatic catclaw fire that almost ruined my face, but I hasten to point out that he took cheap and unfair advantage of the situation.

See, my mouth was full of T-bone, the very same bone he had just tried to steal only moments before, and with my mouth full of T-bone, I wasn't able to defend my honor in the manner . . .

Man alive, I had almost forgotten how much damage a sniveling little cat could do in a very short period of time. He buzzsawed my whole face, fellers, and we're talking about lips, eyebrows, cheeks, gums, nose, the whole shebang.

At that point I abandoned the path of reason, dropped the bone, and went to Total Warfare. If Kitty Kitty had been just half a step slower, he would have paid dearly for his crimes. Instead, I

had to settle for a moral victory: I ran him all the way to the water well and chased him up a tree.

"There!" I yelled at him in a voice filled with righteous anger. "And let that be a lesson to you."

He grinned down at me from the tree. "Yes, I've learned a valuable lesson, Hankie. Chewing on a dog's face is a lot more fun than chewing on a bone. Let's try it again some time."

I tried to think of a stinging reply, but my face and nose were stinging so badly by then . . . I mean, he had really trashed my face, the sneaking little weasel . . . I failed to come up with a stinging reply, so I whirled around and marched away, confident that I had won another huge moral victory over the cat.

At least I had a bone to show for my efforts. Pete had nothing but a tree.

Holding my trashed face at a proud angle, I marched proudly down to the . . . my goodness, there was Sally May at the yard gate. Acting on instinct, I altered my flight plan and pointed myself towards the gas tanks.

I mean, there is something about Sally May that arouses certain feelings of, well, guilt in a dog. Even when we haven't done anything naughty, her very presence makes us think we have. And in this case, I had more or less been involved in chasing her precious kitty . . .

"Hank, come here."

Uh oh. There it was. She had seen everything. She knew everything. She always saw and knew everything. Didn't she ever sleep?

I altered course again and headed for the yard gate, but this time I switched everything over to Looks of Remorse and Mournful Wags. I began rehearsing my story.

"Sally May, I know what you're thinking. You probably think that I was beating up on your stupid . . . that is, you probably think I was fighting with your cat, and I realize that the, uh, evidence looks pretty damaging, but I think I can explain everything. Honest. No kidding."

That's as far as I got with my story. I couldn't seem to get past the "I can explain everything" part. I would just have to wing it and hope for the best.

I approached her with a big cowdog smile. She did not return the smile. Instead, her eyes were filled with ice and snow and cold north winds. Yikes, it appeared that I was in deep trouble.

But you'll never guess what she said. I was shocked. Here's what she said, word for word.

"Now, you look at his face, Alfred Leroy. You see what you caused? Poor old Hank was just minding his own business until you drew him into a fight."

The boy stuck out his lip. "I was only pwaying, Mom."

"I know you were playing, Alfred, but the point is that someone else paid the price for your fun."

"Nuh uh, 'cause Hank and Pete had fun too."

"Maybe they did, but they paid for it. Hank got scratched up and Pete got chased up a tree. And what about you—you who started the whole thing?"

"Well . . . I got scwatched. See?" He pointed to a tiny scratch on his arm. "And it hoorts weal bad, Mom, no foolin'."

She shook her head. "I think you need to come inside and stand in the corner for thirty minutes."

"Aw Mom!"

"And think about being kinder to animals. God didn't put them here for you to torment."

"Aw Mom!"

"In the house. March!"

The boy twisted his face into an angry pout and beamed a hot glare at me, of all things. "Hank, you got me in twouble and you're a dummy."

Me? What . . . ?

I stared at him in disbelief as Sally May escorted him into the house. He was calling ME a dummy and accusing ME of getting him into trouble? What a wild imagination he had!

But that didn't matter now, because Sally May had sniffed out the real culprit in the case and was hauling him off to jail. It served him right, the little snipe.

Justice had been . . . although I had to admit, in the deep dark wickedness of my heart, that giving the cat his daily thrashing had been worth all the scratches. If given the opportunity to do it all over again, I would have done it all over again . . . especially if Little Alfred got blamed for it.

Heh heh.

Not a bad deal, in other words, especially when you considered that I had also won the Grand Prize of three juicy delicious T-bone steak bones, speaking of which . . .

Where were my bones?

I sniffed the ground and located the spots where they had been—three distinking locations that still held the warm and wonderful fragrance of steak juice.

The smell was there. The bones were not.

They were gone.

SOMEONE HAD STOLEN MY STEAK BONES!

I went streaking down to the gas tanks. I had supposed that I would find Drover asleep on his gunnysack bed, but I was shocked to find him awake. But that was only the first of several shocks that awaited me, as you will see.

I came roaring up to the gas tanks, throttled down, hit Full Air Brakes, and came sliding to a stop.

"Drover! I'm glad you're awake."

He gave me his usual silly grin. "Thanks, Hank. I'm glad too, 'cause the awaker you are, the dayer it seems."

"What?"

"I said . . . well, let me think here. I said, the awaker the day, the shorter the night. I think that's what I said."

"Hmmm. Well, that's an interesting way of putting it, but what was your point?"

"The point. Well, let's see here." He rolled his eyes around. I tried to remain patient.

Are you getting impatient? Let's change chapters. Maybe that will help.

C H A P T E R

4

HERE'S A FRESH CHAPTER

There, we've changed chapters. Drover was pondering my question, if you recall. At last he gave his answer.

"The point is that if you sleep all the time, there's not much difference between day and night. I guess."

"I see. There's a certain amount of truth in what you say, Drover, but allow me to point out one small flaw in your ointment."

"Pigs say 'oint.'"

I stared at the runt. "No, as a matter of fact, they don't say 'oint.' They say 'oink,' oink with a K. It's a well-known fact that pigs and hogs are unable to pronounce T's."

"Aw, you're just teasin'."

"Not at all, Drover. It's scientific truth that pigs and hogs . . . "

"What's the difference between a pig and a hog? I've always wondered."

"Then it's good that you asked, Drover. That's how we learn and expand our minds, by inquiring about things we don't understand."

"Yeah, and I don't understand why water is always so wet. And how come chickens move their heads when they walk. We dogs don't walk that way."

"That's correct, Drover, and you've made an interesting observation there."

"Yeah, but what's the answer?"

"The answer is very simple, as most answers tend to be. Your ordinary chicken moves his head when he walks because his head is connected to his legs. Do you know about clocks and pendulums?"

"No, I've never had a clock."

"Drover, I'm aware that you've never had a clock. Even if you had a clock, you couldn't tell time."

"Yeah, if I could tell time, I'd tell it to speed up, 'cause I sure get bored sometimes."

"Yes, well, the source of your boredom is yourself, Drover. It's a well-known fact that boring personalities suffer from boredom."

"I'll be derned. I knew it was something."

I began pacing back and forth in front of him, as I often do when I am plunged into deep thoughts.

"Yes, if you would concentrate on being less boring, you would be less bored. It all fits together."

"Yeah, and you know what? I chewed on a board one time and got splinters in my mouth."

"There, you see? That's exactly my point. Chewing on boards is a way of relieving boredom, but it provides only temporary relief because it doesn't go to the root of the heart."

"I'll be derned. You mean hearts have roots?"

I couldn't help chuckling at his nativity. "Drover, of course they do. Trees have roots. Teeth have roots. All things that are rooted in reality have roots."

"What about root beer?"

"Inside every glass of root beer, Drover, there lurks a root."

"How come it lurks?"

"It lurks because . . . because you ask so many stupid questions, and I'm afraid we're out of time."

"Oh darn. I wanted to ask about the chicken who swallowed the clock."

All at once my lips rose into a snarl, and I found myself glaring at him. "The chicken didn't swallow a clock, you meathead, and stop talking. I came

30

down here on a very important mission and you've got me so scrambled, I can't remember what it was."

"I love scrambled eggs."

"Hush! Not one more word."

"Okay."

My snarl turned into a growl. "You just said one more word."

"I did?"

"Yes, you did. I told you not to say one more word, and you said okay. For your information, okay is one word."

"I thought it was two letters."

"No, it's one word, and I forbid you to say one more word."

"O.K."

"That's better." I began pacing again. My brains had turned into a junkyard. "Now, where was I— and don't answer, Drover. I'm asking myself, not you."

"Okay."

"It was something very important, a problem that absolutely couldn't wait and had to be addressed immediately."

"Well, if 'O.K.' is two letters instead of one word, maybe the two letters have to be addressed."

I stared into the vacuum of his eyes for a long moment. I remembered the two letters that Slim and Loper had addressed and put into the mailbox.

Did Drover know something about that puzzling event, something that he wasn't telling? Was this a clue that promised to lead my investigation off into an entirely different direction?

"Drover, let me ask you one question. Do the letters I-R-S mean anything to you?"

"Well, let's see here. I-R-S. I are confused. 'Confused' starts with an S, so maybe that's what it means."

"'Confused' starts with a C, Drover."

"Gosh, I guess I'm confuseder than I thought."

The breath hissed out of my chest. Suddenly I felt that I was being crushed by the weight of my job, the weight of the investigation, and above all, the weight of Drover's dingbat questions.

And his answers too. His dingbat answers were just as weird as his dingbat questions.

I marched several steps away, blinked my eyes, took several deep breaths, and tried to clear the sawdust out of my head. Then, in a flash, it hit me.

I whirled around. "I've got it, Drover. I just remembered why I came streaking down here."

"Oh good, 'cause I'd almost forgotten."

"Yes, I had come pretty close to forgetting myself."

"Yeah, and if you forgot yourself, you'd really be lost."

I forked him with a gaze of purest steel. "What?"

"I said . . . well, let's see here." He scratched his right ear. "If you went someplace and forgot to take yourself, you'd be out there all alone. I guess."

"Hmmm, yes, that's true, I suppose, but that's a horse of a different color."

"I got hoarse once. Barked all night. Made my throat raw."

"Drover, hush. I was leading up to a very important point, which is that only moments ago, someone stole . . . "

My gaze fell upon a small pile of something between Drover's paws. I hadn't noticed it until now. "What is that between your paws, Drover?"

"My paws?" His eyes drifted down and settled on the objects. "Well, let's see here."

"They look like bones to me. Three bones."

"Yes, they do. Look like bones. Sure do."

I sniffed the air. "Furthermore, they smell like bones."

He sniffed. "I'll be derned, they do. Smell like. Bones."

"If they look like bones and smell like bones, then by simple logic we arrive at the conclusion that they are . . . what?"

"Uh . . . bones?"

"Very good." I lumbered over to him and stuck my nose in his face. "Three bones, Drover, the exact number of bones that were stolen from me at the yard gate. Is it possible, could it be that you stole three bones from the Head of Ranch Security? From your superior? From one of the few friends you have left in this world?"

"Well, I . . . "

"Because if you did, Drover, then you are a thieving, scheming, traitorous, treacherous little pickpocket."

"Oh my gosh, don't say those things, Hank!"

"It's true, isn't it? Out with it! I want the truth, the holey truth, the awful dreadful truth. Go ahead and confess, Drover, before it's too late."

"Well . . . " He was so shook up, I thought he might start crying. "All right. I confess."

"I knew it, I knew it!"

"I confess that I saw . . . a Bone Monster!"

An eerie silence moved around us. I stared at the runt. I could hardly believe my ears. The words had gone through me like a bolt.

"What did you just say?"

"I said . . . when?"

"Just now. Repeat what you just said."

"Oh, okay." He rolled his eyes and wadded up his face in an expression of . . . something. Great concentration, I suppose, or total confusion. I couldn't tell. At last he spoke. "Was it something about clocks and chickens?"

"No."

"Hogs and pigs?"

G.L.Holmes

"No. You were confessing, Drover, and you said something about a . . . a Bone Monster."

"Oh yeah. What a scary guy!"

I marched a few steps away. "Drover, I've been on this ranch for many years and I've never seen or heard of a Bone Monster. I don't mean to doubt your word, but tell me more. Did you actually see this . . . this thing steal my bones?"

"Oh yeah, you bet, saw it with my own eyes."

I sensed that the interrogation was entering a critical phase, so I told him to sit down and relax, while I stalked back and forth in front of him.

I mean, this was pretty serious stuff. A Bone Monster, on my ranch? I had to get to the bottom of this.

C H A P T E R

5

DROVER'S SHOCKING STORY

Interrogating a nitwit requires just the right technique, don't you see. It's not as easy as you might suppose.

"All right, Drover, we're entering the Factual Phase of the interrogation. In ordinary language, that means we're searching for the facts, only the facts."

"Oh good."

"Question: Where did you see this so-called Bone Monster?"

"Well, let me think here. He was up by the yard gate."

"Hmmm. That checks out. What did he do that made you think he was stealing my bones?"

"Well, he stole your bones."

"That checks out too. How many bones, Drover?"

"Three."

"Describe the Bone Monster."

"Well, let's see here." He closed one eye and twisted his mouth. "He was big. And shaggy. And looked like a gorilla, a big shaggy gorilla."

I marched several steps away, gathering my thoughts. Suddenly I whirled around. "All right, Drover, I can reveal that we've run your story through our files at Data Control and it checks out. We're now convinced that you're telling the truth."

"That's weird."

"What?"

"I said, oh good. Oh boy. I'm so happy."

"Exactly. Now that we've cleared the first turtle, we'll zoom in for more specifics and finer details." I studied him out of the corner of my eye for a moment. "Drover, there's just one part of your story that doesn't mash. You have told this court that you saw the Bone Monster in the act of stealing my bones, is that correct?"

"I think that's what I said."

"That IS what you said."

"Oh good, 'cause that's sure what I wanted to say."

"Great. But there's a missing chink in the puzzle. If the Bone Monster actually stole my bones, how did you end up with them?"

"Oh gosh, that's a good question. Did you think it up yourself?"

I studied the claws on my right paw. "Oh yes, I handle all these interrogations myself, and coming up with probing questions is just part of my job."

"Boy, you did a great job."

"Well thanks, Drover. It's kind of you to say that. A lot of dogs wouldn't have noticed."

"Yeah, it was a great question. I really enjoyed it."

"Good. That's . . . hmmm, I seem to have lost my train of thought. Where were we?"

"Well, let's see here." He yawned. "I think you'd just asked me about the weather."

"Yes, of course. How's the weather been, Drover?"

"Oh, pretty good. Not too hot and not too cold." He yawned again. "We could use another rain."

"Am I boring you? You keep yawning."

"No, sometimes I yawn, that's all." He yawned. "See?"

"Yes, I saw that. But back to the weather, it's getting dry, isn't it?"

I waited for his answer. When it didn't come, I swung my gaze around just in time to see his eyelids slam shut. I was about to awaken him with a thunderous roar—I mean, after all, the little dunce had fallen asleep while Court was in session, and sleeping under oath is one of the many things I don't allow on this ranch.

But I caught myself just in time. You see, a plan had begun to form in the darkest outskirts of my mind. It suddenly occurred to me that the bones were sitting there, unwatched and unguarded.

And they were, after all, MY bones. I had won them, fair and square, in a scuffle with the cat, and gathering information about the Bone Monster could, uh, wait.

I wasn't sure I believed his story anyway. I mean, who ever heard of a Bone Monster?

I cut my eyes from side to side. No one was watching. On silent paws, I crept over to the pile of bones, loaded them up in my enormous jaws, and we're talking about all three at once, and crept away from the gas tanks on padded paws that made not a sound.

Ten feet away, I shifted into a rapid walk, then into a trot, and finally into an easy gliding lope. And whilst I was doing all this, my mind was racing. Where would I deposit this treasure of bones?

G.L. Holmes

I considered a list of secret locations and rejected all but one for the same reason: The ground was hard and I hate to dig. Having shrunk my list of options down to one, my decison became very easy.

I would deposit my treasury of bones in Sally May's garden, for her husband had tilled it up just weeks before. Perhaps in some strange manner, known only to women, she had perceived that her loyal dog would soon need a soft place to bury some precious bones.

They are very perceptive, you know. The ladies, that is. Sometimes they seem able to read minds and forecast the future. It's called Women's Institution, and it can be pretty spooky.

Well, if Sally May's institution had caused her to plow up the garden just for me, it seemed totally right that I should accept her act of kindness. I mean, she was probably aware that digging in hard ground will dull a dog's claws, and that sharp claws are very important to the, uh, overall security program of the ranch.

It all fit together. Only one obstacle stood in my way. The alleged garden was enclosed inside a hogwire fence, but it happened that hogwire fences were no big deal to me. Clenching my enormous jaws around the bones, I went into a deep crouch, took a huge gulp of air, and launched myself into the air.

Charge! Banzai!

BONK.

Okay, we had forgotten about that strand of barbed wire above the hogwire. What we had was four feet of hogwire with the single strand of barbed wire above it, and that small fact had altered all our careful calculations and equations and so forth.

It was no big deal, it could have happened to any dog, and it merely etched another mark into a nose that had already been etched by the stupid cat.

And by the way, those had been lucky punches.

Anyways, I made contact with the almost-invisible top wire and took a rude tumble to the ground. OOF! Knocked the breath out of me for a second, but I'm no quitter. I reprogrammed all of the launch data, sank into another deep crouch, and went flying over the top like a . . .

Tomato plant? It appeared that she—Sally May, that is—she had not only tilled the garden but had also set out some tomato plants, so to speak. Nobody had informed me of this, and it's very hard to operate a ranch when nobody tells you anything.

They expect us to know everything, and they're very quick to pass out blame when a small mistake is made, but ask for current information and everybody's too busy to file their reports.

But the important thing was that I had made it into the garden area and had wrecked only one of Sally May's tomato plants. One or two. Several. But it was a small price to pay for a successful mission, and I knew that Sally May would understand.

I mean, those bones were a very precious cargo.

Once in the garden area I set up shop and went to work. I dug a hole in the soft dirt near the northeast corner, dropped the first precious bone into it, and covered it up with my . . . well, with my nose.

Why do we dogs dig holes with our paws and cover them up with our noses? I've seen it happen over and over, and it's always the same. To be perfectly honest, I don't understand it but I do it very well, so maybe it doesn't matter.

I mean, if you can do it, who cares if you understand it? And if you understand it but can't do it, what's the point?

The point was that I buried the first bone, then hurried on and buried the other two, following the exact same procedure: digging with paws, covering with nose.

On completing the third and final bone deposit, I paused to rest a moment, to gaze out upon a job well done and . . .

Suddenly the silence was shattered by a voice coming out of nowhere!

Hey, I had thought I was all alone in the world— just me and my precious buried bones and the warm glow of a job well done. But hearing the voice behind me, I knew that I was not alone in the world.

The voice startled me, jolted me, so to speak, out of a dreamy state of mining. I jumped, twisted my entire body to the left, and heard myself deliver a kind of gurgling growl. It wasn't my best growl, I'll admit, but very few of us are at our best in such awkward moments.

The important thing is that I did manage to fire off a growl or two before . . . well, landing in the

midst of another tomato plant. And, yes, maybe I transplanted a few sprigs of lettuce.

She had—Sally May, that is—it appeared that she had planted a few rows of lettuce, but of course nobody had turned in that report either, and when they don't turn in their paperwork, how am I supposed to know where the silly lettuce is planted?

Who can run a ranch when he has to tiptoe through the tulips and lettuce and tomatoes? We have to keep the Big Picture in mind, don't you see, and . . .

I turned all my sensory equipment toward the sound of the voice, half expecting to see a huge shaggy . . . okay, relax. It was Slim. He was leaning on a fencepost.

Grinning at me.

6

I BREAK THE TRAGIC NEWS
TO DROVER

Have you noticed that Slim always seems to be leaning on something? It's true. He never stands up straight on his own two legs. He leans.

This could be caused by simple laziness. I've suspected for a long time that Slim is, at heart and down deep where it really counts, a lazy man.

Or perhaps his body is crooked, and it just naturally falls into a slouching state whenever he is at rest—which is fairly often, if you ask me. If they ever gave me full authority to run this ranch, I would . . . but never mind that.

He was draped over the corner post and he was grinning at me. "Hey pooch, has anybody ever told you that you've got mud on your nose?"

I . . . there wasn't a simple answer to that question. Of course I knew that mud existed on the end of my nose, but technically speaking, nobody had ever pointed it out before.

But I was aware of it, and I was also aware of why it was there.

"Have you been playing backhoe with your nose?"

No, I certainly had not . . . okay, maybe I had done some backhoe-type work with my nose, but I hadn't been PLAYING. It was very serious business. Heads of Ranch Security don't PLAY.

We WORK, which was a concept he wouldn't understand.

"You know, Hank, only your best friends would tell you this, but you look pretty silly, standing there with a mudball on the end of your nose."

I held my head at a proud angle and glared daggers at him. Not only was I not ashamed to have mud on my nose, I was proud of it. So there.

Small minds will always find something to ridicule. Ridicule, I guess it should be, something to ridicule.

When you do serious backhoe work with your nose, it becomes muddy, and that was nothing to ridiculate.

He chuckled to himself and started walking toward the machine shed. "Well, if I was you, pup, I believe I'd get out of that garden. Sally

May's liable to take a dim view of you plantin' bones in the midst of her tomater plants."

I had to admit that he had . . . gee, was it so obvious that I had . . . that a strong wind or something had blown down a plant or two? Maybe so, and yes, leaving the garden area before certain parties arrived seemed a pretty good idea, even though the idea had come from one of the smaller minds on the ranch.

You probably think that I left the garden right then. Not true. First, I scanned the entire garden area and committed to memory the locations of all three of my precious bones.

See, a lot of your ordinary ranch mutts will go to the trouble of burying a bone and then leave. Only later will they realize that they have no idea where they left it. That falls into the category of Dumb Behavior.

If you're going to bury a bone, doesn't it make sense to remember where you left it? Of course it does. That's what I did, and then I made a rapid exit, so to speak, from the scene of the, uh, accident.

I felt pretty bad about the damage, but history has proven over and over that if you're going to make an omelet, you have to break a few tomatoes.

On the other hand, I've heard Sally May and other leading experts on gardening say that tomato plants actually do better after they have been "flailed," I believe they call it.

Flailed or frailed or flogged. Whipped. Beaten. Thrashed with a stick. No kidding. Some people whack on their tomato plants with a stick, so in a sense, you might say that I had actually helped Sally May with some of her, uh, gardening work.

Hey, I was glad to do it. Sally May was a very busy wife and mother, and she had no business thrashing tomato plants in the hot glare of the sun's hot glare.

I made my way back to the gas tanks. Drover was just as I had left him, conked out—snoring, wheezing, twitching, grunting, and doing all the other things he does in his sleep.

I sat down and watched him for a few minutes. Did I make such noises in my sleep? I didn't think so. I also took this opportunity to figure out how I would break the sad news to him. At last I came up with a plan, which began with a gentle wake-up call.

"Wake up, half-stepper, arise and sing!"

Well, you won't believe this. I hardly believed it myself, and I was there and saw the whole thing. Before my very eyes, the little mutt arose and sang. Here's now it went, and he sang it more than once, if you can believe that.

The Wake-up Song

Murgle skiffer porkchop on a
   summer day.
Skittle rickie snicklefritz eat a bale
   of hay.
Elephants.
Sugar ants.
Steak fat snork.
Porkchop mork.

I listened to the entire mess. As far as I knew, Drover had done very little singing in his lifetime, and it certainly showed. It was pretty bad.

I cleared my throat. "Excuse me, but unless I'm badly mistaken, you are not only sleeping in the middle of the day, but you're also singing on the ranch's time."

His eyes came into focus and that silly grin of his slithered across his mouth. "Oh hi, Hank. You've got a mudball on the end of your nose."

"Oh yes, I . . . uh . . . " I turned away and swiped my nose with a paw. "Thanks. I can't imagine how it got there."

"Maybe you were digging."

"Don't be absurd, Drover, and don't try to change the subject. The point is that you were singing on ranch time."

"Me? I was singing?"

"That's correct, on the ranch's time and during business hours."

"I'll be derned. I can't even sing."

"I noticed. Now brace yourself, Drover. I have some terrible news."

"I don't think I can stand it. I just woke up and you know how I am in the morning."

"It's not morning, son. The day's half over."

"No, it's still morning. See where the sun is?"

I beamed him a glare. "Do you want to argue the time of day or hear some terrible news?"

"I think I'd rather argue. I hate terrible news. It always seems so terrible."

"Exactly, and there's a reason for that. Terrible news seems terrible because it is. Now sit down and be quiet and brace yourself. I have to tell you something."

He sat down and braced himself. "How terrible is it?"

"Be quiet and you might find out."

"Okay." He squeezed his eyes shut. "What if I can't stand it?"

"That's why I told you to sit down. When you can't stand something, you should sit."

"Oh. That makes sense. I guess I'm ready."

"Very well, here we go. Drover, it's my unpleasant duty to inform you . . . "

"That's enough, I can't take anymore!"

"I haven't told you anything yet, you little weenie."

"Yeah, but it's already so bad that my leg's starting to hurt. Maybe you could start with the good news first."

"All right, we'll try it your way. The good news, Drover, is that your bones have disappeared."

His eyes popped open. His jaw fell several inches. "That's not good news, that's terrible news!"

"I'm sorry, son. I had to trick you."

"Yeah, but you tricked me."

"That's what I just said, Drover, but I tricked you for your own good. Somebody had to trick you into facing reality as it really is."

"I want to go back to bed. I want my bones. Oh, my leg!"

I gave him a pat on the shoulder. "I know this is hard on you, Drover, but there's more." I looked into his eyes and lowered my voice to a whisper. "For you see, Drover, your bones were stolen by . . . the Bone Monster."

His eyes grew as wide as saucers. "You mean . . . he was here?"

"That's correct."

"The Bone Monster was HERE?"

"Exactly."

"While I was asleep?"

"I've run out of ways of saying yes, Drover, but yes, all those things you have said are true and correct."

"Oh my gosh!" He sat down and began scratching his left ear with his left hind leg. (I notice all these tiny details.) "Tell me what happened."

"All right, let's see here. I was giving you an important lecture on . . . something. I don't recall the subject matter at the moment."

"Yeah, it was pretty boring and I fell asleep."

I beamed him a hot glare. "Do you want to tell this story or shall I?"

"No, you better do it, 'cause I don't know what happened."

"Fine. I'll tell the story and you concentrate on being quiet. You fell asleep. I left to do a quick sweep of the corrals and feed barn. On my return, I was astonished to see this . . . this creature standing in your bedroom."

"Oh my gosh, what did he look like?"

"Just as you described him, Drover: a huge, hairy, shaggy, gorilla-type creature."

"With red eyes that blinked on and off?"

"Exactly."

"And long fangs?"

"Same guy."

His teeth had begun to chatter. "Oh my gosh, Hank, it must have been the Bone Monster!"

Pretty scary, huh? You probably think there wasn't a Bone Monster, that I was just making it up. That's what I thought too, but you'll soon find out . . .

You'll see.

CHAPTER

7

DOGPOUND RALPH APPEARS ON THE SCENERY

I had Drover's full attention. "What did he do?"

"Well, let me think. Oh yes, he looked down at you and licked his chops, almost as though . . . almost as though he were thinking of . . . eating you, Drover."

"Oh my gosh, it's a good thing I didn't wake up. I'd have died, Hank, just died! What did he do then?"

"Well, he didn't eat you."

"Oh good!"

"Instead, he saw the three bones between your paws. He glanced over both shoulders, snatched them up with a big hairy hand, and lumbered off to the northwest."

By this time, Drover had crawled underneath his gunnysack bed. Nothing showed but his stub tail. "Where do you reckon he went, and do you think he'll come back?"

"I'm guessing that he went to Spook Canyon, Drover. That's about the spookiest place on the ranch. And as to whether he'll be back . . . we just don't know the answer to that one."

I could see the gunnysack shaking. "I'll never be able to sleep again, not with him running around."

"I guess the next question is, do you want to send a scout patrol into Spook Canyon and try to recover your bones?"

He poked his nose out the west side of the gunnysack. I could just barely see one of his eyes. "Who'd be in the scout patrol?"

"The entire massed forces of the Security Division, Drover. Or to put it another way . . . you."

His nose and eye vanished. "You know, Hank, the way this old leg's been acting up, I probably better stay close to the gas tanks."

"Mmmm yes, that's what I thought."

"And Bone Monsters have to eat too, just like the rest of us, and maybe if he has steak bones to eat, he won't want to be trying to eat us."

I caught myself smiling. "Good point, Drover, I hadn't thought of that. So what you're saying is that you're willing to drop the whole thing and not file charges in the case?"

"Oh yeah, you bet. I was never so happy to lose three bones."

Bingo! Heh, heh. My net worth had just zoomed into the statusphere. I was now the sole owner of three of the best bones in Texas. And Drover was happy about it. What a deal.

"Well, whatever you think, Drover. It's your life and they were your bones. And by the way, you can come out now. The Bone Monster left thirty minutes ago."

His nose appeared. "Oh, I think I'll stay in here for a while longer, just in case. My leg needs a rest anyway."

"Fine, but I'll expect you to be ready for Night Patrol. We'll move out at 1800 hours sharp."

"Night Patrol! What about the Bone Monster?"

"Sure, invite him to come along. The more the merrier."

"Oh my leg!"

I left him quivering under his gunnysack and went on about my business. I felt great. It was a beautiful spring morning and I had three wonderful bones in the bank. What more could a dog ask of this old life?

I headed up the hill, past the yard gate, past the machine shed, through the shelter belt, and onward and northward to the county road. It had occurred to me, don't you see, that I hadn't worked Traffic in several days, and that was too long.

I hate to let Traffic slide, but sometimes it can't be helped. I get so busy with investigations and monster reports and so forth that I can't do a thorough job with Traffic. And I always regret it.

I mean, when you skip a few days of barking cars on the county road, those guys get to thinking it's THEIR road and they'll start driving like mechanics . . . .maniacs, I guess it is . . . they start driving like maniacs, hogging the road, expending the seed limit, and disregarding all our rules and regulations.

Well, you know where I stand on those issues. I don't allow 'em, and the sooner those guys figure it out, the happier we'll all be.

Imagine my surprise when I topped that little hill north of the house and saw two unidentified pickups parked on the side of the road . . . MY road, that is. They appeared to be just sitting there, using my road as a parking lot, and I guess you know that we don't allow such things, especially when the guilty parties don't have permission.

The farther I went, the madder I got. Those guys would pay dearly for this. Even though I had just made a killing in the bone market and was now a fabulously wealthy dog, I was in no mood to be generous. By George, if they wanted a free parking space, they could go somewhere else.

As I drew closer, I began sifting clues and memorizing tiny details. It was two pickups, all right, one red and one white. The red one was parked behind the white one, and the driver of the red one had gotten out and was standing beside the white one.

They appeared to be talking—the drivers, not the pickups. The drivers appeared to be talking. I could hear the low murmur of their voices. That was a pretty important clue right there. They were *murmuring*.

Why would two drivers of two pickups be murmuring to each other on the side of a county road on a pretty spring day? It struck me as pretty fishy, and I had every intention of getting to the bottom of the barrel.

Fifty yards out, I fired off a warning bark. Sometimes that will send them fleeing in terror. I mean, once they realize that they've been caught in the act by the Head of Ranch Security, a lot of these loafers and deadbeats will quit the country, never to be seen again.

That's not what they did. Instead, they . . . well, I couldn't see that did much of anything, actually, which provided me with another important clue: Those guys had no idea who or whom they were fixing to go up against. And maybe they weren't real smart on top of that.

By this time, I had abandoned all hope of settling this in an easy or peaceful manner. Obviously, I would have to kick tails and take names and maybe even tear a few doors off of a few pickups.

I hated to be so drastic about it, but some guys just don't take hints.

I rumbled up to the first pickup, which happened to be the red one in the rear. The rear of the pickup was red but so was the front. It was red all over, in other words, but it . . . phooey.

I rumbled up to the second pickup in line. I chose it at random, for no particular reason. As far as I was concerned, one was just as guilty as the other.

Without wasting a single second of my time, I marched straight to the right rear wheel and proceeded to mark it with Secret Encoding Fluid. Once we have SEFed a tire, we feed the secret coding information into Data Control. For days and weeks thereafter, we can call up a SEF Report and trace the location of every tire of every vehicle we have SEFed.

Pretty snazzy, huh? Maybe you thought this was a sharecropper outfit, staffed by a couple of dimwit dogs. Ha! Far from it. Over the years, we have upgraded our equipment and brought in the very latest up-to-date high-tech instruments that help us in our never-ending battle against . . .

Who or whomever it is that we're against. The villains of this world. The slackers and the trespassers, cattle rustlers and roadhogs, and the list goes on and on.

On most of your ordinary ranches, your ordinary ranch dogs merely mark the tires. Not us, fellers. We encode them with Secret Encoding Fluid and . . .

Suddenly and all at once, I had a feeling—a strange creepy feeling—that I was being watched.

I rolled my eyes upward. Sure enough, there was the face of a dog, staring down at me. While continuing to SEF the tire, I began memorizing every detail of the alleged face.

How many dogs can do both those jobs at once? Very few. It requires tremendous powers of concentration, because if you happen to get the two tasks mixed up . . . well, it could lead to water on the brain.

I lifted my eyes and here's what I saw: two big sad eyes, one mouth, one nose, two long floppy ears. If I had been forced to give a quick analysis of the face, I would have guessed that it belonged to some kind of hound dog, either a bassett or a beagle.

I finished up the SEF procedure, scratched up some gravel with my front paws, (that gravel-scratching seems to help "set" or "fix" the Encoding Fluid), and turned my full attention to the trespasser in the pickup.

I broke the long icy silence. "You seem to be staring at me, fella. Is there some reason for that?"

"Well, I was just a-wondering what you were doing down there, I guess, is why I was staring. Are you wettin' down the tires?"

"It may appear that's what I'm doing, but in fact of actuality, it's quite a bit more complicated than that."

"Oh. Well, I probably wouldn't understand it then. I'm kind of slow."

"Hmmm, yes." I had already picked up that clue, that he was "slow," to use his word, and suddenly I had the feeling that . . . "Say, pal, haven't we met before?"

"Yup, sure have. Name's Ralph. They call me Dogpound Ralph 'cause I stay at the dog pound. You visited me twice at the pound."

I began pacing. "Yes, of course. It's all coming back to me now. Don't you see what this means? You're Dogpound Ralph!"

"Well . . . that's what I thought."

"Yes, yes, of course. I knew I'd seen you before: your face, the mournful eyes, the drooping jowls.

G. L. Holmes

They all add up to YOU, Ralph, and they will never add up to anyone else."

"Good. I reckon."

"You might recall, Ralph, that I'm the guy who broke you out of prison and saved you from a miserable existence as a jailbird."

"Yup, either that or I broke you out, 'cause you had just eat a bar of soap."

"No, you're wrong, Ralph. I had been poisoned by my enemies. They had plotted to poison me with a deadly hydrophobia virus."

"It was soap, ya dope. Your sister fed you soap 'cause you wouldn't take a hint and go home."

Would I just stand there and take this kind of insult from a jailbird dog who was trespassing on my ranch?

You'll soon find out.

C H A P T E R
8

MISS SCAMPER FALLS
MADLY IN LOVE WITH ME

We glared at each other for several seconds. Then I broke the icing and walked a few steps away.

"Okay, Ralph, have it your way. So what brings you down here?"

He began scratching his left ear with his left hind leg. I waited. He was a slow scratcher.

"Me and Jimmy Joe Dogcatcher are going to camp out at the lake and fish all night."

My eyes fell on two fishing rods in the cab. "Hmm, yes, that fits."

He stopped scratching and looked at me. "Did you ask was I having fits?"

"No, I did not. I said, 'that fits.'"

"Oh. I thought . . . can't hear so good when I'm scratchin'." He went back to scratching. "Did I mention that there's a lady dog in that white pickup?"

My eyes popped open. Suddenly I was wide awake. "What? A lady dog? You mean I've been listening to you all this time and there's a lady dog only fifty feet away?"

"Uh huh. I wanted to go talk to her, only I'm too bashful. I'm always afraid they'll laugh at my long ears."

I studied his long ears. "They are pretty long, tee hee, aren't they? I mean, I have nothing against long ears, Ralph, but those may be the, ha ha, longest ears I ever saw."

He heaved a deep mournful sigh. "See? That's why I can't talk to the girls. We'd just end up talking about my big ears."

"Those are definitely some amazing ears, Ralph. Do you ever step on them when you walk?"

"Uh huh, all the time. It's pretty embarrassing."

"I'll bet. Well!" I leaped to my feet. "I'll march over to that pickup and give you a few lessons on how to impress the womenfolk."

"Oh good. Can I watch?"

"Sure. Watch and take notes. You might as well learn from one of the best in the business."

I left him there with his big ears and made my way around to the second pickup. Before I got there, I slowed my pace to a manly swagger and let my eyes drift up to the . . .

Mercy! She was a beagle, surely one of the most gorgeous beagles ever to draw a breath. She was looking into the rear glass of the pickup and primping on her face. When I came into view, she saw me in the glass.

"Well, well!" she gushed in a sultry voice. "Mirror mirror on the wall, look who's coming, big and tall! Hello there, big boy."

I sat down and beamed her a rakish smile. And then, in my deepest, most malodorous voice, I said, "Howdy, ma'am. Unless these eyes deceive me, you are the lovely Miss Scamper."

She fluffed up her ears, then turned and came floating over to the tailgate, wearing a foxy little smile. She fluttered her . . . mercy me, she fluttered those long eyelashes and I almost forgot to breathe.

"You're pretty cute yourself, Wolfie. Do we have a name for you?"

"Oh yes ma'am. Hank the Cowbell . . . er, Hank the Cowdog, Head of Ranch Security, at your service, ma'am."

"Oooo. Are we a pretty important dog, is that what we're saying?"

"Well, I'm not one to broast or bag . . . boast or brag, that is, but it's been said that, yes, I'm a fairly important dog."

She studied the claws on her right front paw. "Are we merely important or are we also rich?"

"Ha, ha. Funny that you should ask. As a matter of fact, I recently made a huge fortune in the bone market."

One eyebrow twitched. "Oooo. Little fortunes don't thrill me, but I can be impressed by huge ones."

"Well, I've got one. I also write poetry, speak many languages, and do tricks."

"You're a busy little fellow, aren't you? So what's causing all the dust?"

"Huh? Dust?" It was then that I noticed the small cloud of dust that had risen around us. "Oh, the dust. My best guess, Miss Scamper, is that you've caused my tail to wag extra hard, and it's kicking up a, uh, small cloud of dust . . . so to speak."

She coughed. "That's a pretty smart tail, but maybe we could slow it down, now that we're friends."

"Sure, you bet." I punched in the commands for Relaxed Tail. It didn't work. I shot a glance at Miss Scamper.

She was fanning the air with a paw. "It keeps wagging, doesn't it?"

"Uh, yes ma'am, so it seems. It's been a while since we've had a gorgeous lady on the ranch, don't you see, and the old tail just . . . ha ha, wants to wag, I guess."

She coughed again and gave me a frozen smile. "Maybe we should do a trick."

"Right. Just what I was thinking. Okay, check this one out." I stood up and walked a short distance away, loosened up my enormous shoulder muscles, and prepared for the trick. "Now watch. Bang!"

I fell to the ground and played dead. I laid there for fifteen seconds and didn't even breathe, then leaped to my feet and took a bow.

"Pretty impressive, huh? I'll bet you thought I was really dead."

"I was almost worried sick."

"Great. You want to see another one?"

"If you've got the money, honey, I've got the time."

"You're covered. Watch this one." I hopped up on my back legs and walked around in a circle. Then, before her very eyes, I shifted to only one leg.

Fellers, that was a toughie. To be honest about it, I had never attempted it before, and I'm not sure that any dog in the whole world had ever attempted it. It was that difficult a trick.

I shot her a glance and noticed that her eyes had wandered. Hmmm. This lady was hard to impress, but my next variation on the trick would no doubt leave her breathless.

"Okay, Miss Scamper, watch carefully. This next move will knock your socks off."

It was a backwards flip, if you can believe that. Balanced on one leg, I went into a deep crouch, leaped upwards and kicked my hind legs into the air, and . . . BONK!

The crucial part of the maneuver is getting your back feet over your head and then around on the other side, without breaking your neck in the process. I didn't quite get 'er done, shall we say, and came up with a crooked neck and sand in my mouth.

But the good news was that she was smiling. That made it all worthwhile. Anything to please the ladies, I always say.

"Well! What do we call that one?"

"We call it . . . " I tried to straighten my neck. "We call it the One Leg Hop-Circle, With Half A Flip and A Busted Neck. It's a world-class stunt."

"I'll bet." She fluffed at her ears. "What's next, or is that all?"

"Well, I . . . actually, that was probably my best trick, Miss Scamper."

"Oh shucks."

"But let me hasten to add that I sing."

Her eyes swung around and struck me. "You sing?"

"Right. I sing, as in la-la-la-la. You know, singing. Music. Songs."

"And I'll bet we're fixing to hear one, huh?"

"Oh . . . well, sure, I guess I could do one for you."

"And let me guess. You wrote it yourself, right?"

"Well . . . yes, as a matter of fact, I did. But how did you know that?"

She looked away. "Hon, I've lapped this track before."

"I beg your pardon?"

"I said, let's hear the song."

"Well, sure, if you really . . . here we go."

I'd Like To Be Your Pal

Miss Scamper, we just barely met
    and I'd like to be your pal,
But I'm not the kind of feller who
    gets silly over gals.

See, I'm Head of Ranch Security, I
  call this ranch my own.
I'm used to work and hardship and
  spending time alone.

A lot of dogs will lose their heads
  when a lady comes around.
They'll go to howling at the moon
  and rolling on the ground.
But that's not me, it's not my style,
  I'm more the silent kind.
I hold my feelings deep inside this
  calculating mind.

You've got the prettiest beagle face
  this cowdog's ever seen.
Miss Scamper, you just blow my
  mind, you're every puppy's
  dream.
My heart's about to float away like
  a big old red balloon.
I swear, I'm thinking seriously
  'bout howling at the moon.

Oops, let me get control of things
  before my feelings show.

See, I'm really not the kind of dog
    who wants the gals to know
That I might be impressed at all by
    the way a lady looks.
I try to run this ranch of mine
    strictly by the books.

So don't you expect for me to faint
    and blush and bow . . .
Did you just wink your eye at me
    and arch that lovely brow?
Now cut that out, Miss Scamper,
    I'm trying to stay composed!
Dadgum the luck, I'm a sittin'
    duck, and totally exposed.

You've got the prettiest beagle face
    this cowdog's ever seen.
Miss Scamper, you just blow my
    mind, you're every puppy's
    dream.
You shouldn't have winked that
    eye at me, I'm as crazy as a loon.
To heck with pals, I love the gals,
    I'm howling at the moon.

9

DOCTOR BUZZARD
ARRIVES

When I finished up the song (it was pretty good, didn't you think?), I saw her looking down at me with an odd little half-smile on her mouth.

"What do you think of that, Miss Scamper?"

"Well, it leaves me . . . uh . . . breathless, shall we say."

"Right. Me too."

She fluffed her hair. "I can hardly believe that my little wink could have such an effect on a big old hairy thang like you."

"Yes, right. It's kind of amazing."

"And you say you're rich, huh?"

"Oh yes ma'am, fabulously rich. I hardly know what to do with all my fortune."

Her brows twitched. "I think I can help. I wonder if you could hop your bad self up here in my pickup?"

"You wouldn't think me too bold or brazen?"

She fluttered her eyelashes. "I'll try to keep an open mind."

Heh, heh.

I went into a deep crouch, went flying over the tail gate, and landed right beside her.

She studied me with hooded eyes. "Well, here you are."

"Yes ma'am, here I am."

"That rhymes, doesn't it?"

"It sure does. I hadn't thought of that." A heavy silence moved in between us. "My, this is fun, isn't it?" I began to feel uncomfortable. "I wonder what this weather is going to do."

"I have a feeling that a storm is fixing to hit."

"Oh really? I didn't know you . . . "

It was then that I saw the "storm" she had mentioned. It wasn't a cloud, as you might have thought, but rather the furrowed angry face of her master, whose name was Baxter. Apparently he and Jimmy Joe Dogcatcher had finished their conversation about fishing and were ready to leave.

He had a big black mustache and beady little eyes, Baxter did, and he was glaring at me. "Get out of my pickup, you potlicker."

I heard my claws scratching the bed of the pickup and I went sailing over the tailgate. I landed in a heap in the ditch. It was a little embarrassing, to tell you the truth, but hey, that guy had caught me by surprise and . . .

I saw her looking back at me as the pickup pulled away. Her eyes were filled with sadness

G.L.Holmes

and adoration, and I knew that her heart was about to break.

"Goodbye, Miss Scamper! We had our precious moments together and now we must part. Until our hearts are reunited, you must try to be brave."

Her eyes seemed to roll upward, and I heard her exclaim in a voice filled with sadness and adoration, "Oh brother."

Ah, what sweet words! I would carry them with me forever and ever . . . or at least for a little while. Anyways, she vanished into the sunset . . . sunrise . . . over the next hill and I was left with a huge hole where my heart used to be.

Jimmy Joe Dogcatcher had fired up his pickup and was pulling away, heading west towards the lake. I saw Ralph's head hanging over the tailgate. I turned on a burst of speed and caught up.

"Did you see that, Ralph?"

"Yup."

"That's how you charm the ladies. The tricks softened her up and the song finished her off."

"She looked kind of bored to me."

"Bored? You don't understand the ladies, Ralph. They try to hide their emotions."

"Well, she done that, all right."

"But in fact, she fell madly in love with me, and I would bet that, at this very moment and even as we speak, she's crying her eyes out."

"I'll bet she's fixin' her hair."

"Exactly, and learning to cope with her broken heart."

"Oh brother."

"What? I'm falling behind, Ralph, and I guess I'll have to sign off. Goodbye, old friend, my old prison buddy."

"See you around, Harry."

"It's Hank, Hank the Cowdog. Come back again some time and I'll give you some more tips on charming the gals."

"Or whatever."

"Goodbye!"

"So long."

I slowed to a walk and watched him pull away. It was kind of a touching moment, saying goodbye to an old prison . . .

He fell out!

The driver swerved to miss a chughole in the road, and Ralph fell out the back and landed in the ditch. His ears flew in all directions and he rolled all the way out into the horse pasture.

And there he lay . . . motionless.

Fearing the worst, I rushed to his side. "Ralph, speak to me. It's your old prison buddy, Hank the Cowdog. You've just been involved in a serious accident. I think you're going to be okay, but you need to speak to me. Say something. Ralph?"

Nothing. He didn't speak or move. I began pacing.

"Ralph, I'm feeling personally responsible for this. If I hadn't tried to carry on a conversation with you while the pickup was moving, this never would have happened. I feel terrible about it.

"So would you please wake up? If you won't wake up for yourself, wake up for me. Think of somebody besides yourself for a change. What am I supposed to do now? I mean, I can't just walk away and leave you out here all alone in the pasture. I could never forgive myself.

"But the other side of that, Ralph, is that I'm a very busy dog. I've got a ranch to run, and by the way, it just occurs to me that my Bone Fortune needs to be checked. You see, we've had reports of a Bone Monster on the ranch . . . "

I gazed down at him. He still hadn't moved. I lowered my right ear to his nose and listened. Yes, he was breathing.

I sat down and began what I feared would be a long virgil. Vigil. I sat down and waited for something to happen.

Nothing happened. The minutes crawled by. I hate waiting. It drives me nuts. I was just about at the end of my rope of patience when, suddenly and all at once, my ears picked up the sounds of flapping wings.

I turned to the left and saw two big black airplanes coming in for a landing. Good grief, they must have been enemy bombers, diving down for low-level . . .

Okay, relax. They weren't enemy bombers. They were buzzards, two of 'em.

The first one touched down, rose again, touched down again with a thud, did three forward rolls, and got up running. He came straight over to me and my injured companion.

He was dragging his wings and yelling. "Git back, step aside, make way for Emergency Airborne Medical Services!"

The second buzzard crash-landed several feet away and rolled into a cactus patch. The sight of these two crazed birds dropping out of the sky left me speechless.

The first one came right up to my face—and let me tell you, fellers, that was one of the ugliest things I'd seen in a long time.

He was yelling again. "I'm Doctor Buzzard, Emergency Airborne Medical Services. We've been called to the scene of a wreck. Where's the victim?"

I pointed to Ralph. "That's him on the ground. His name's Ralph."

"Son, we don't care what his name is. The boy's been hurt and that's why we're here. Junior, bring me my bag, and hurry, first chance you git."

G.L. Holmes

Okay, it was Wallace and Junior, but I'd never known them to do anything like this before. It appeared that they had come to . . . well, help, if you can believe that. It seemed a little out of character, but we did need help so . . .

Junior came limping up. "W-w-w-we d-didn't bring a b-b-bag, P-pa." He saw me there and waved his wing. "Oh, h-hi D-ddoggie."

"How's it going, Junior?"

"Oh, b-b-busy b-b-busy. W-w-we're w-working wrecks today, today."

"Yes, I see that. Is this something new for you guys?"

"Oh w-w-well, P-p-pa just thought w-w-we'd . . ."

Wallace's head flew up. "Son, quit talkin' with the customers and give me a hand. Where's my bag?"

"W-w-we d-don't h-h-have a b-bag, P-p-pa, and n-never did, never did."

"Fine. We don't need a bag. What matters is all this knowledge inside our heads. Get yourself in here and check this dog's vital signposts. We ain't got a minute to spare."

"P-pa?"

"What!"

"I l-l-landed in a c-c-cactus b-b-bush."

"And did you get spines and needles in your hide?"

"Y-y-yep, I d-d-d-did, and they sure h-h-hurt."

Wallace puffed himself up to his full height. "Son, haven't I warned you about driving too fast? Speed kills, Junior, and the speedier you drive, the killier you get, and one of these day's you'll wake up dead, is what's liable to happen."

"Yeah, b-b-but . . . "

"And son, it serves you right, crashin' into a cactus bush, and maybe that'll teach you to slow that thing down. Now get in here and take his vital signposts."

The two of them hovered over Ralph's potsrate form. I watched, hoping for the best.

"Okay, Junior, how 'bout his hoofbeat?"

"Y-y-you mean heartbeat?"

"Whatever. Give me something, and hurry. Supper's a-waitin'."

"W-w-well, I c-can't f-feel much through m-my f-f-feathers."

"In other words, he ain't got a heartbeat. How about breathing? Is he breathing?"

"W-w-well . . . "

"Snake-eyes on that too, huh? How 'bout blood pressure?"

"W-well, if h-his h-heart ain't b-b-beating, P-pa, then h-he c-c-an't have a . . . "

"I read the book too, Junior, so you don't need to be showing off like you're an I-don't-know-what, 'cause you ain't." There was a moment of silence. Then Wallace's head came up. "Boys, I'm afraid we've lost him."

CHAPTER
10

THE CHUCKIE CHIPMUNK EPISODE

Those words went through me like a duck out of water. Ralph and I had gone down many happy trails together, but now . . . The tragic expression that had etched itself on Wallace's ugly face suddenly vanished. All at once he didn't look sad at all.

"And now, pooch, it's time for you to run along. Me and Junior will take care of all the arrangements."

"Wait a minute, hold on. Since when were you involved in emergency medical work?"

"Since I started chasin' wrecks, is since when— if it's any of your business, which it ain't. Now run along home."

I gave him a stern glare. "I don't think so, Wallace. If you're a doctor, my name is Lulu."

"Then your name is Lulu, 'cause I got my doctor's license from the Buzzard School of Medicine and Mortuary. We save the ones that can be saved and recycle the rest."

I was about to go to sterner measures when Junior said, "P-p-a, I th-think h-he's w-w-waking up, waking up."

Wallace spun his head around to Junior. "Who's waking up? Where's he at? What are you trying to say?"

He pointed a wing at Ralph. "The, uh uh, v-victim. Our p-p-patient."

"Son, I already told you. He's gone. We lost him. It's a terrible tragedy but he didn't die envaned. We ain't had but rabbit scraps in three . . . "

Just then, old Ralph sat up and blinked his eyes. His gaze went from one buzzard to the other. He swallowed hard.

"Well, Ma always said I'd end up here, if I didn't change my ways, and here I am. Darn."

Wallace shrank back as though he'd seen a ghost, but it didn't take him long to recover.

"There, you see that, pooch? Emergency Airborne Medical has saved another life, yes we have, and you had the gall and the nerve to . . . Junior, we have done our job and we can be proud, very proud of our selfless devotion to duty, but life goes on and so does the rent on this stomach of mine. Let's get back in the sky and find us a better wreck somewheres else."

I couldn't help chuckling. "See you around, Doctor Buzzard."

"You better believe it's Doctor Buzzard, and don't you forget who saved that friend of yours and snatched him back from the very edge of the grave, and your name is Lulu. So there!"

They taxied into the breeze and began flapping their wings and rose into the sky.

"P-p-pa, I've g-g-ot c-c-cactus in m-m-my a-a-armpit."

"Son, buzzards ain't got armpits 'cause we ain't got arms."

"W-w-well, okay, th-then in m-my w-w-w-w-wingpit."

"Son, I told you and told you. If you don't slow that thing down and stop driving like thirty-three drunk monkeys . . . "

I didn't hear the rest of the sermon, which was just fine. There's very little a buzzard has to say that I need to hear. I turned my attention to Ralph, who was staring at me with glazed eyeballs.

"Where am I? How many fingers am I holding up? Who's on first?"

"Take it easy, pal. You had a serious accident but you're going to be all right. Do you remember who you are?"

"Sure. I'm Chuckie Chipmunk and Miss Scamper's in love with me. And your name's Lulu. And I just bailed out of an airplane but my parachute didn't open."

"Uh . . . listen to me. Your name's Dogpound Ralph. You fell out of the back of a pickup and landed on your head. You're suffering from a medical condition called Milk of Amnesia. It will pass, so don't panic."

"I'm Chuckie Chipmunk."

I heaved a sigh. "Fine. You're Chuckie Chipmunk."

"I'm a big chipmunk, aren't I, Lulu?"

"Yes, you're one of the biggest chipmunks in the world."

"You reckon I could get a job in the circus?"

"Sure. There happens to be a circus right over there." I pointed towards ranch headquarters. "Let's hike over and see if they're hiring . . . overgrown chipmunks."

This conversation was kind of crazy, but I had decided to play along with him until his head cleared.

We started walking. I noticed that Ralph had a hitch in his get-along, but that was no surprise. He had taken a nasty fall.

He broke the silence. "You reckon they'll have elephants in the circus?"

"Oh sure. I'll introduce you to one."

"Oh good. When I was little, I wanted to be an elephant."

"No kidding? What stopped you?"

"Well, I was already a chipmunk, and once you're a chipmunk, you can never be an elephant."

"Of course. I should have known. But tell me this, Ralph."

"Chuckie. Chuckie Chipmunk."

"Sorry. Tell me this, Chuckie. You mentioned Miss Scamper. Is she a chipmunk too?"

"Nope. She's a beaver, only she was wearing a dog suit to disguise herself. Pretty smart, huh?"

"Oh yeah. You bet."

Was there a pattern here? If so, I couldn't find it. It appeared to me that Ralph had lost his marbles. I just hoped he would find them again. One weird dog on the ranch was about all I could stand.

I'm speaking of Drover, of course.

We made it into headquarters and I led him over to the storage tank, next to which we had a pan of fresh water. I told him to drink. He did. When he was done, he ran his tongue over his lips to sop up the drips.

He was quite a drippy drinker. I had picked up that clue right away.

"Well, Chuckie, how are you feeling now?"

He glanced around. "Who you talkin' to? My name's Ralph, Dogpound Ralph, and I'm supposed to be fishin' with Jimmy Joe."

It appeared that the water had cleared his head. Did I dare try to explain the business about Chuckie Chipmunk? I decided to skip it. It was getting along towards sunset and I had things to do.

I suggested that he stay the night at our place and strike out in the morning to find his master. We had plenty of room under the gas tanks and he could share my gunnysack. Or Drover's. Yes, we had plenty of room and he could certainly share Drover's gunnysack.

"Come on, Ralph, I've got some very important business to take care of before dark, and you might as well tag along."

He followed me down the hill, past the old cellar, past the overflow of the septic tank, through that grove of big elm trees, and to the gate of Sally May's garden. Here, I stopped and glanced around in all directions, to see if we had been followed.

Everything looked normal, but just to be on the safe side, I lowered my voice to a whisper. "Ralph, you may not realize it, but on the other side of that fence lies a fortune in buried bones."

His ears jumped and he licked his chops. "I sure love bones, especially ones that have been aged."

"Yeah, well, we need to talk about that, Ralph. Since you're here as a guest, I don't mind giving you a peek at the bones, but only if you swear never to reveal the secret. Do you solemnly swear?"

He did.

"Good. Now, the next challenge, Ralph, is that we have to scale this hogwire fence. Watch me and then we'll give you a shot at it. Here I go."

I made a giant leap upward, hooked my front paws over the top wire, dragged and heaved the rest of my body over the top, and tumbled over the other side.

Ralph watched this with his big bassett eyes, then gave his head a shake. "Can't do it. I think I'll just use the gate."

I laughed at his ridiculous statement and . . . hmmm . . . watched as he nosed the gate open with his . . . well, with his nose, of course, and came padding into the garden.

I beamed him a glare. "For your information, this is a Secured Area and that gate wasn't supposed to be unlatched."

"Uh huh, but it was."

I made a mental note of this clue, little realizing that it would soon become a very important detail.

I glanced over both shoulders, just to be sure we hadn't been followed, then made a dash to the northeast corner of the garden. There, I began a furious digging process to unearth the first of my

Precious Bones. I dug so hard and so fast, I didn't realize that I was spraying Ralph with dirt.

"Reckon you could point that dirt somewheres else?"

"No, but you can always move."

"Too much trouble."

"Fine. Sit there and eat dirt. I'll be finished in just a second." At that very moment, my claws scraped against something solid. "Ah ha, here we are. Wait until you see this bone, Ralph. You'll be . . . "

HUH?

I stared at the object I had just unearthed with my furious digging. It wasn't a precious T-bone. It was a . . . you won't believe what it was, so I won't even bother to tell you.

My heart sank. I couldn't believe this was happening to me. I went plunging across the garden to the northwest corner and began digging in Location #2. I already had begun to suspect what I would find there, but I had to know for sure.

I was right.

Little needles of fear moved down my spine. I found myself noticing every shadow and every sound around me, and also that darkness was falling fast. My body wanted to run away and leave this place, but my mind prevailed. I had to know what lay in that third hole.

I swallowed my fear, my growing sense of dread, and ran to Location #3. I dug with the energy of a maniac, until at last I heard my paws make that familiar sound.

I gazed into the hole. My bone was GONE, and in its place I saw . . .

I turned to Ralph. "Ralph, I don't want to alarm you, but we've got a Bone Monster running loose on this ranch. My guess is that he's watching us at this very moment. On the count of three, we will run for our lives. One!"

Ralph was already gone. He didn't wait for two or three. And you know what? Neither did I.

CHAPTER

11

THE BONE MONSTER
TURNS OUT TO BE REAL

I mean, if a guy's life's in danger, if he's being watched by a horrible red-eyed Night-Stalking Bone Monster, why should he stick around for the full count?

We didn't, fellers. We went into Rocket Dog Mode and got ourselves out of that creepy place. I never would have dreamed that Ralph could run so fast on those stubby legs of his, but he was picking 'em up and laying 'em down.

We went streaking to the gas tanks. Drover had been sleeping, but his head came up as he heard the roar of our rocket engines and the screech of our brakes.

His ears were crooked and his eyes were crossed. "Mirk snork snicklefritz, who's that?"

I was panting for breath. "Drover, this is Dog-pound Ralph. Ralph, meet Drover, my assistant."

G.L.Holmes

They exchanged nods while I caught my breath. "Drover, I'm afraid we're in for one of the longest and scariest nights of our lives."

His face wilted. "I don't think I want to hear this."

"I'm sorry, son, but it's my duty to tell you the facts."

"I hate facts, especially scary ones. Oh Hank, don't tell me that it's the Bone Monster."

I stared at the runt. "How did you know? Did you see him too?"

"Well, I . . . "

"That makes two of us who caught a glimpse of him. How about you, Ralph? Did you see him too?"

"Well . . . I saw something."

"There you are! That makes three out of three. We all saw the Bone Monster, so there's no question that he's on the loose, out there somewhere in the black darkness of night."

Suddenly I heard an odd sound. Then I realized that it was coming from Drover. His teeth were chattering.

"Drover, do something about your teeth."

"I can't take 'em out. What should I do?"

"I don't know, but stop clicking them." I began pacing back and forth in front of my troops. "All right, men. I feel it's my duty to give you all the information in this case."

Drover moaned. "I don't think I can stand it!"

"Hush. As you already know, the Bone Monster entered our Garden Vault and stole all three of our bones."

Drover stared at me with empty eyes. "Garden Vault? What . . . I thought . . . I think I missed something."

"Exactly, which is why you should pay attention once in a while. But the crucial fact here is that, after stealing my . . . that is, our bones, the Bone Monster LEFT SOMETHING IN THE HOLES."

I heard Drover gasp. "You mean . . . "

"Exactly. He stole the bones and left a carbolic object in their place. Bone Monsters always do that. It's part of their routine, their pattern."

There was a long throbbing silence. Then Drover said, "Gosh, I wonder what he left."

I stopped pacing and whirled around. "I'll tell you what he left, Drover. In each of the holes, he left . . . a Vienna sausage can. Do you see what this means?"

"Not really."

"It's very simple, if you understand the mind of crinimals and monsters. They take something of great value—a bone, for example—and leave something that contains a secret coded carbolic message. Ralph, would you care to guess the secret carbolic message of an empty Vienna sausage can?"

"Well . . . let me think."

I waited. Time was slipping away. "I'm sorry, Ralph, but we're out of time. The secret carbolic message is . . . " My eyes flicked back and forth, from one terrified face to the other. "The secret message is that the Bone Monster intends to *make sausage out of us.*"

Drover keeled over. "Oh my gosh, I'm too young to be a sausage, and this old leg is killing me!"

"Get up, Drover, this is no time to show your true colors. It happens that I have a plan. We'll make our stand here at the gas tanks. We'll need someone to stand guard. I'm looking for a volunteer."

No paws went up, so I turned to Ralph. "How about it, Ralph? You've had valuable experience as a jailbird. You just might be the right dog for this job."

"I don't think so. We don't have monsters at the dog pound, and besides, my legs are so short, I'm kind of nearsighted."

"Hmmm. I hadn't thought of that. How many fingers am I holding up?"

He squinted at me. "Let's see. Fifteen?"

I turned to Drover. "Ralph's out. I guess it's down to you and me. Or to put it another way, Drover, congratulations. You get the job."

"Yeah, but I saw fifteen fingers too. My eyes are terrible."

"They'll get better with practice."

"And this old leg of mine . . . "

"Never mind the leg, Drover. You'll take the first watch. Ralph and I will go into Bunker Position. If you see anything suspicious, you can give us a call."

Drover whimpered and cried, but I ignored him.

By the time Ralph and I entered the Fortified Bunker, darkness had fallen over the ranch. Oh, and in case you're not familiar with Fortified Bunkers, let me describe this one. It consisted of one gunnysack. To enter the bunker, we eased our heads beneath the sack.

You may not believe this, but that layer of gunnysack material provides excellent protection against, oh, incoming mortar shells, laser beams, you name it. It also has the extra benefit of shutting out a world that has become . . .

How can we put this? If a guy needs a break from the rigors of . . . he can find peace and quiet beneath a gunnysack, is the point.

I know, Drover often uses this technique to flee from Reality, but that's a different deal.

Anyway, Ralph and I entered the Fortified Bunker. He broke the long silence. "You reckon the monster'll come back?"

"We don't have an answer to that, Ralph."

"I wish I was fishin' with Jimmy Joe."

"Get some sleep, Ralph. This may be a long night."

"I wish I was back at the dog pound. I wish . . . "

Just then Drover called in his first report. "Hank, I see something out there!"

Ralph and I froze. Perhaps we exchanged worried glances. It was hard to tell in the darkness of the bunker. I decided to break radio silence.

"Blue Moon, this is Dishpan. Go ahead."

"I was calling for Hank. I must have got the wrong number."

"This is me, you drip, but I'm running under the code name Dishpan. Your code name is Blue Moon. Go ahead, Blue Moon. What do you see?"

"Well, I'm not sure, but it moved."

"Roger, Blue Moon. Keep your eye on it and let us know what happens, over."

There was a minute or two of eerie silence. Then . . .

"Blue Dish, this is Moonbeam. It's still out there, and it's still moving."

"Roger, Blue Moon. Can you identify that odd noise we're picking up?"

"It's my teeth again."

"Roger, Blue Moon. We'd better go to Silent Teeth. Can you give us a description, over?"

"They're long and white and smooth."

"What are you describing, Blue Moon?"

"My teeth, and I can't keep 'em still."

"Blue Roger, Moonshine, but we need a description of the moving object, over."

"Oh. Well, let's see here. Oh my gosh!"

"What is it, Blue Moon? Report at once, over."

"It's a . . . he's . . . oh my gosh! Dishrag, this Blue Cheese, and it's a . . . it's a red hairy gorilla with three yellow eyes and huge claws and long bloody teeth and . . . and he's seven feet tall and he's . . . CRUSHING BONES IN HIS MOUTH!"

That last part sent a jolt of electricity out to the end of my tail. I tried to remain calm, but that wasn't easy.

"Holy cats, Drover, you've just described a Bone Monster."

"I was afraid of that. What should I do?"

"Hang on, Cheese Ball. Give us a minute to think." I sent an urgent message to Data Control.

Data Control sent back meaningless signals. We were on our own now. "Swiss Cheese, this is Grease Rag. What's the situation now?"

"I want to go home!"

"What's the Bone Monster doing, over?"

"Well, let me see. He's . . . oh my gosh, he's coming this way and he's . . . he's grinding his teeth together and he's . . . he just said he wants to eat a COWDOG!"

Yikes.

I switched off the radio and turned to Ralph. "Ralph, are you there?"

"Uh huh, and if I ever get out of here alive, I ain't ever leaving the dog pound again."

"How fast can you run?"

"Well, usually not too fast, but I think I can feel a burst of energy comin' on."

"Good. We're surrounded. We've got to make a run for it. Drover, we're coming out."

"Are you talking to me?"

"Of course I'm talking to you!"

"I thought I was Cheese Ball. I'm all confused."

"Drover, do you want to be confused or do you want to run for your life? You can't do both."

"I'll take Number Two."

"Fine. Then quit squeaking nonsense. We're coming out." We came flying out of the bunker. My eyes probed the darkness around us. "Where is he, Drover? Give me exact coordinates."

"Well, first he was over there, then he moved over here."

"Is that longitude or latitude?"

"I think so. Anyway, he was huge and ugly."

"Got it." I faced my little band of troopers. "Okay, men, we've got to bust out of here. It's our only chance. We'll make a run for the yard gate, regroup there, and scale the fence."

Drover spoke. "I ate a fish scale once. Couldn't swallow for a whole day."

"Exactly, so on this mission we must avoid all fish and swallows. Are we ready to move out? Let's make a run for it, and don't speak to any strangers. Good luck, men."

And with that, we ran for our lives.

12

I UNMASK
THE BONE MONSTER

We fought our way up the hill. Boy, what a scary deal it was. See, our intelligence reports had spoken of only one Bone Monster out there, but by the time we reached the yard gate, I was pretty sure that we had encountered more than one.

Several.

Dozens of Bone Monsters, each one bigger and meaner and uglier than the first one.

Pretty scary, huh? You bet it was.

Well, our squad had been encircled and entrapped by a whole bustallion of Bone Monsters. They were everywhere! I mean, in the darkness up ahead, we could see their yellow neon eyes flickering on and off.

And you probably think they were fireflies, but they weren't. I know a firefly when I see one.

These were the murderous yellow eyes of a whole bunch of Bone Monsters.

Ten feet out, I knew we were in big trouble. We would have to fight for every step, every inch of ground.

"Okay, men, I had hoped that we could make this a silent run, but they've got us surrounded and outnumbered. When I give the word, we'll go into Heavy Duty Barking."

"What's the word?"

"The word, Drover, is 'bark.' What else would it be?"

"Well, I don't know. Blue Cheese or Hamburger Bun or Lettuce Leaf. You use all these codes and sometimes I don't know what's going on."

"Yes, but what's more important is that THEY don't know what's going on. It's all part of a grand strategy and you don't need to worry about it. Just bark." He barked. "Not yet, you moron, you'll give away our location."

"They can have it! I want to go home, and this leg is killing me!"

"Okay, men, ready on the left? Ready on the right? Commence Heavy Duty Barking! Give 'em the full load and don't hold anything back!"

We cut loose with a withering barrage of barking. Boy, you should have heard us! I was especially

G.L.Holmes

impressed with Ralph's work. He was a hound dog, you know, and hounds have always been good barkers.

His was a deep "Roof, roof" which added some force to Drover's yips and squeaks. And then, of course, I weighed in with my deepest and most threatening bark, which is probably what saved us.

We ran a few steps, stopped and barked back the waves of attacking Bone Monsters, then ran a few steps more. It was brutal.

At last we made it to the yard gate. We had fought and clawed our way through the Enemy lines, through wave after wave of suicidal Bone Monster attacks, and somehow we had made it.

I was proud of my guys. You never really know what a dog is made of until he's . . .

The door? The back door was opening? Thank goodness, we had awakened the house and someone was coming to our rescue!

I heard a voice in the darkness. It was Loper's.

"If you idiots wake me up one more time, you're going to be eating buckshot." Gulp. "Do you hear me, Hank?" Yes sir. "Now shut up your barking!"

Yes sir. I knew from past experience that Loper wasn't a totally rational person in the middle of the night. There were many things he didn't understand about Security Work, and I could only hope that, come morning, he would see the arrow of his ways.

And yes, I understood the message about "buckshot" and knew that he wasn't kidding.

The door slammed shut and the lights went out in the house. I turned to my companions. "Nice work, men, but we're not quite finished. Our final objective is to capture and defend the back porch. Any questions?"

Ralph raised his paw. "I can't climb this fence, legs are too short."

"In that case, Ralph, go down fighting, and take a few monsters with you. It's been a real pleasure knowing you."

His ears jumped. "Last one to the porch is a rotten egg."

And then, before our very eyes, he climbed over the fence. It wasn't very graceful, but he got 'er done. Drover went over next, while I covered the rear, and then I went soaring over the fence like a deer.

That rhymes, doesn't it? Rear and deer. And it also reminded me of the lovely Miss Scamper and the many perfumed hours we had spent together—reciting poetry, singing songs, staring into each other's eyes. What a gal, and she was madly in love with me.

By the time I reached the porch, Drover and Ralph had already set up in the Back Door Security Formation, and they had done it on their own, without any prompting from me. I was proud of them. My guys were really coming through in the crutch.

Oh, in case you're not familiar with BDSF, here's a quick outline of the procedure. It calls for the dogs to sit down on the porch and press their backs as tightly against the door as possible. This not only stops all traffic in and out the door, but it keeps the house from moving around.

It also makes us feel that we're almost inside the house, which is pretty important on scary nights.

I took my place in the BDSF pattern. "Well, guys, we made it. Nice going. We won't get any sleep tonight but at least . . . " My ears picked up the sounds of their snoring. "Ralph? Drover?"

They were both sound asleep—sitting up, mind you. Well, that was okay. They had fought a brave fight, and as their commanding officer, I didn't mind taking the entire nightwatch mysnork. I was wide awoink by then and snicklefritz porkchop murgle . . .

Perhaps I dozed, but not for long. The next thing I knew, it was daily broadlight. A crazy person was standing on the other side of the screen door, whomping on us with the door and screaming incoherent messages about . . . something.

"Will you get off my porch and let me out of my house? And what are you doing in my yard!"

HUH?

My eyelids lifted. My eyeballs rolled around three times in their sprockets, then focused on a certain cat-like figure sitting in the iris patch. It was a cat. It was Pete.

He appeared to be bathing his left hind leg with a pink tongue, and he was grinning. "Hi, Hankie. Walk in your sleep last night, hmmm?"

I beamed him a look of coldest steel. "No, I didn't walk in my sleep last night. For your information, Kitty, my men and I . . . "

Where were they? Ralph and Drover had vanished. I was alone on the porch, and that same crazy person was still whamming me with the . . .

Okay, it was Sally May. I whapped my tail on the porch and gave her my warmest, most sincere good-morning . . . oof! . . . smile, and if I moved off the porch, maybe she would stop . . . oof! . . . hammering me with the screen door.

I moved. She came out, placed her hands on her hips, and leaned over until her nose and my nose were only inches apart. I wondered if a nice juicy lick on the nose would, uh, heal this latest wound in our relationship, so to speak.

I decided to save the lick for another time.

Our eyes met. "You barked all night long."

Yes, but I could explain . . .

"You woke up everyone in the house."

There were these Bone Monsters, see, these dreadful horrible Bone Monsters, and Drover and Ralph and I were just minding our own business and . . . where were those two jugheads anyway?

"And here you are," she continued, "in my yard. Dogs are not allowed in my yard, ever. And do you know why?"

I, uh . . . no. It seemed a very strange law to me.

"Because I saw what you did to my tomato plants, you oaf, and if I ever catch you in my garden again . . . "

I didn't hang around for the threats. I shot one last glare at Precious Kitty and ran for my life.

Sally May just didn't understand. If she had only known about the attack of the Bone Monsters and the Sausage Death Threat . . . oh well.

Part of being a dog is learning to forgive.

I was not shocked on finding Drover and Ralph asleep under the gas tanks. I gave them a rude awakening.

"A fine bunch of comrades you are, slipping away in the night and leaving me to be scorched by Sally May! What do you have to say for yourselves?"

Ralph staggered to his feet and gave his head a shake. "What I have to say is that I'm leavin'. I never knew what a nice place the dog pound was 'til I came out here." He started walking west, towards the lake. "Bye, y'all, I'm going fishin'."

"Hey Ralph, is that it? No thank-yous or good-byes?"

"Thanks and goodbye. Blue Cheese, buckshot, Bone Monsters, baloney. A guy could get killed trying to sleep on this outfit."

"Well, goodbye, old pal, old prison buddy. Come back again some time."

He disappeared from sight and I turned an angry glare on Mister Vanish. "Drover, I hardly know what to say."

"Oh good."

"After all our years of service together . . . "

At that very moment, Drover was saved from a blistering lecture because Slim had just pulled up to the gas tanks in his pickup. He stuck the gas nozzle into his tank and gave us a big lazy grin.

"Morning, dogs. My pickup was down to fumes, and I reckon I'd better finish my breakfast before Loper starts shoutin' orders." He reached in the window and pulled out an open can of . . .

I stared at the can. Drover stared at the can. We exchanged long thoughtful glances.

He was eating VIENNA SAUSAGE. From a CAN.

My mind raced back to the previous day. I was burying bones in the garden, right? Slim was there, watching me and making cute remarks about . . . something about a backhoe, right? And he was a big joker, right?

The pieces of the puzzle began . . .

He popped a weenie into his mouth and grinned. "Have you checked on your bones, Hankie?"

HUH?

Okay, maybe we had . . . he thinks he's so funny, and sometimes I wish . . .

G.L. Holmes

Never mind. The important thing is that I had solved the Mystery of the . . . phooey.

Case closed.

And he didn't fool me with that business of the Vienna sausage can, not for a minute. And don't forget who came up with the first report of the Phony Bone Monster.

It was Drover.

I'd never believed that Phony Bone Monster stuff. No kidding.

Case closed, forever this time, and don't go blabbing this around either.

Have you read all of Hank's adventures?
Available in paperback at $6.95:

Also available on cassettes:
Hank the Cowdog's Greatest Hits!

THE COWDOG's
Security Squad
WANTS YOU!

Be a Deputy Head of Ranch Security! We'll send you a special collector's box filled with neat stuff, including:

- **An interview** on audio cassette with author John Erickson
- **An autographed photo of** John Erickson
- **A big full-color Hank poster**

- **2 Official Hank bookmarks**
- **2 Security Squad stickers**
- **More cowdog goodies**

You'll also get a coupon for a FREE book, tape, or gift pack when you buy one of equal value. That's a value of up to **$24.95** for your 2-year membership dues of only **$8.95** plus $2 shipping and handling.

MORE SAVINGS FOR SQUAD MEMBERS

Deputies get THE HANK TIMES 4 times a year. It's packed with the latest news, stories, fun games, contests, and SPECIAL DISCOUNTS.
